Hispanic Heritage

Hispanic Heritage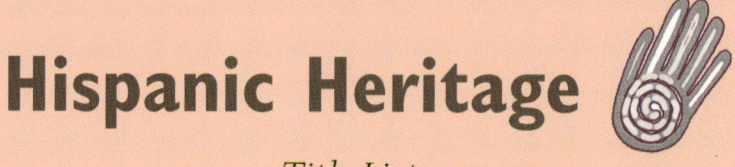

Title List

Central American Immigrants to the United States: Refugees from Unrest

Cuban Americans: Exiles from an Island Home

First Encounters Between Spain and the Americas: Two Worlds Meet

Latino Americans and Immigration Laws: Crossing the Border

Latino Americans in Sports, Film, Music, and Government: Trailblazers

Latino Arts and Their Influence on the United States: Songs, Dreams, and Dances

Latino Cuisine and Its Influence on American Foods: The Taste of Celebration

Latino Economics in the United States: Job Diversity

Latino Folklore and Culture: Stories of Family, Traditions of Pride

Latino Migrant Workers: America's Harvesters

Latinos Today: Facts and Figures

The Latino Religious Experience: People of Faith and Vision

Mexican Americans' Role in the United States: A History of Pride, A Future of Hope

Puerto Ricans' History and Promise: Americans Who Cannot Vote

South America's Immigrants to the United States: The Flight from Turmoil

The Story of Latino Civil Rights: Fighting for Justice

Latino Cuisine and Its Influence on American Foods

The Taste of Celebration

by Jean Ford

Mason Crest Publishers

Philadelphia

Mason Crest Publishers Inc.
370 Reed Road
Broomall, Pennsylvania 19008
(866) MCP-BOOK (toll free)
www.masoncrest.com

Copyright © 2005 by Mason Crest Publishers. All rights reserved. No part of this publication may be reproduced or transmitted in any form or by any means, electronic or mechanical, including photocopying, recording, taping, or any information storage and retrieval system, without permission from the publisher.

13 12 11 10 09 08 07 06   10 9 8 7 6 5 4 3 2

Library of Congress Cataloging-in-Publication Data

Ford, Jean.
  Latino cuisine and its influence on American foods : the taste of celebration / by Jean Ford.
     p. cm. — (Hispanic heritage)
  Includes bibliographical references and index.
  ISBN 1-59084-935-3 ISBN 1-59084-924-8 (series)
  1. Cookery, Latin American—Juvenile literature. I. Title. II. Hispanic heritage (Philadelphia, Pa.)
  TX716.A1F67 2005
  641.598—dc22
                          2004016006

Produced by Harding House Publishing Service, Inc., Vestal, NY.
www.hardinghousepages.com
Interior design by Dianne Hodack and MK Bassett-Harvey.
Cover design by Dianne Hodack.
Printed in the Hashemite Kingdom of Jordan.

Contents

Page 7
Introduction

Page 9
1. Immigration: Creating Change

Page 31
2. Inception: Reaching Regions and Restaurants

Page 43
3. Innovation: "Fusing" Foods

Page 51
4. Ignition: Fiery Fast Foods

Page 65
5. Inundation: Broadening the Beverage World

Page 75
6. Infiltration: Alluring Alcohol

Page 85
7. Influence: Hitting Home

Page 106
Timeline

Page 107
Further Reading

Page 108
For More Information

Page 109
Index

Page 112
Biographies / Picture Credits

Introduction
by José E. Limón, Ph.D.

Even before there was a United States, Hispanics were present in what would become this country. Beginning in the sixteenth century, Spanish explorers traversed North America, and their explorations encouraged settlement as early as the sixteenth century in what is now northern New Mexico and Florida, and as late as the mid-eighteenth century in what is now southern Texas and California.

Later, in the nineteenth century, following Spain's gradual withdrawal from the New World, Mexico in particular established its own distinctive presence in what is now the southwestern part of the United States, a presence reinforced in the first half of the twentieth century by substantial immigration from that country. At the close of the nineteenth century, the U.S. war with Spain brought Cuba and Puerto Rico into an interactive relationship with the United States, the latter in a special political and economic affiliation with the United States even as American power influenced the course of almost every other Latin American country.

The books in this series remind us of these historical origins, even as each explores the present reality of different Hispanic groups. Some of these books explore the contemporary social origins—what social scientists call the "push" factors—behind the accelerating Hispanic immigration to America: political instability, economic underdevelopment and crisis, environmental degradation, impoverished or wholly absent educational systems, and other circumstances contribute to many Latin Americans deciding they will be better off in the United States.

And, for the most part, they will be. The vast majority come to work and work very hard, in order to earn better wages than they would back home. They fill significant labor needs in the U.S. economy and contribute to the economy through lower consumer prices and sales taxes.

When they leave their home countries, many immigrants may initially fear that they are leaving behind vital and important aspects of their home cultures: the Spanish language, kinship ties, food, music, folklore, and the arts. But as these books also make clear, culture is a fluid thing, and these native cultures are not only brought to America, they are also replenished in the United States in fascinating and novel ways. These books further suggest to us that Hispanic groups enhance American culture as a whole.

Our country—especially the young, future leaders who will read these books—can only benefit by the fair and full knowledge these authors provide about the socio-historical origins and contemporary cultural manifestations of America's Hispanic heritage.

Latino Cuisine

1

Immigration: Creating Change

Piñatas at Toys "R" Us . . .
ATMs in English or Spanish . . .
Breakfast Burritos at McDonalds . . .

Unless you've lived in a cave over recent years, you've probably noticed increasing signs of Latino influence in every aspect of American life. Ricky Martin hits reverberate on teens' MP3 players. Tacos add spice to school menus. Salsa is no longer just a Latin music style. Antonio Banderas has become a movie heart-throb, and J. Lo needs no defining. ("Jennifer Lopez," for you cave dwellers!)

Artwork
Latino art is rich with color and flare—and so are Latino foods.

Latino Cuisine

A small bodega sells Latino foods.

The Latino invasion is impacting every nook of American culture. Look at TV: ESPN unveiled its new network "ESPN Deportes" in January 2004, complete with Spanish-language SportsCenter. *Brothers Garcia* is a hit sitcom on Nickelodeon. Discovery en Español, CNN en Español, VHUno, HBO Latino, and MTV en Español are just a few of many Spanish-speaking offerings in mainstream media. Even the History Channel announced the debut of "The History Channel en Español" in May 2004.

If viewing habits don't convince you, how about speech? Spanish is by far the most common foreign language taught in American classrooms. Many company phone recordings instruct, "If English, press one. *Por Español, dos.*" Words like *sí, gracías, mañana, olé, adiós, El Niño, La Niña, señorita, piñata, sombrero,* and *fiesta* roll off even the most foreign-language-challenged tongues. Then there's the immortalized, "Hasta la vista, baby" (Arnold Schwarzenegger, *The Terminator,* 1984).

From TV to music, books to movies, fast-food to groceries, even banking and electronics, Latino influence on U.S. culture is huge and undeniable. American taste buds are no exception. This book explores the effect our southern neighbors have had on American eating habits, including their impact on the fast-food industry, sit-down restaurants, home eating and entertaining, grocery shopping, vending machines, and beverages. But first, let's clarify terminology.

ethnic: relating to large groups of people with a common racial, national, or tribal background within a larger, usually dominant, society.

You Say Hispanic, I Say Latino

You might be wondering why we're using the term "Latino" rather than "Hispanic." Hispanic is an older term that traditionally referred to people and things connected to Spain and/or the Spanish language. It's an English word made up by English-speaking people who applied it to a spectrum of *ethnic* groups, many of which happen to speak Spanish.

"Latino," on the other hand, is an existing Spanish word. (It even has gender: a man is a Latino; a woman, a Latina.) The more general application was coined by Latin Americans living within the United States—it originated within their community—and refers to all peoples from any part of Latin America, whether or not they speak Spanish.

purists: those who want something in its unchanged form.

Many Latinos also identify themselves by country of origin. For example, people with roots in Colombia might prefer "Colombian" over "Latino." Those from Chile might identify themselves as Chilean; folks from Ecuador, as Ecuadorian; from Brazil, as Brazilian; from Puerto Rico, as Puerto Rican; from Mexico, as Mexican; and so on. Yet, they're all Latino. Hence "Latino" refers to a general culture, not one, specific nationality.

Latin America

Chili peppers are an important ingredient in Latino foods.

What countries are considered Latin American? Well, not even Latinos themselves can agree. Some **purists** say only those Western Hemisphere countries that speak Spanish are considered Latin American (Cuba, Puerto Rico, Dominican Republic, Mexico, Nicaragua, Costa Rica, Guatemala, El Salvador, Honduras, Panama, Venezuela, Colombia, Ecuador, Peru, Bolivia, Chile, Argentina, Uruguay, and Paraguay). Other Latinos include Portuguese- and French-speaking countries, too (for example, Brazil and Jamaica). For the sake of this book, we've applied the most common understanding of the term; we include Spanish-speaking nations.

The determining factors, then, are these:

1. that the countries lie in the Western Hemisphere south of the United States
2. Spanish is the primary language.

According to our definition, Latin America includes Mexico, the countries of Central America, most of the countries of South America, and many Caribbean islands.

One last note on terminology: by "Latino influences," we

Latin American Cuisines

The *Directory of World Cuisines* lists these distinct cuisines as Latin American:

Argentine (Argentina, South America)
Belizean (Belize, Central America)
Bolivian (Bolivia, South America)
Caribbean (Caribbean Islands)
Chilean (Chile, South America)
Colombian (Colombia, South America)
Costa Rican (Costa Rica, Central America)
Cuban (Cuba, Caribbean Island)
Dominican (Dominican Republic, Caribbean Island)
Ecuadorian (Ecuador, South America)
Guatemalan (Guatemala, Central America)
Guyanese (Guyana, South America)
Honduran (Honduras, Central America)
Mexican (Mexico, North America)
Nicaraguan (Nicaragua, Central America)
Panamanian (Panama, Central America)
Paraguayan (Paraguay, South America)
Peruvian (Peru, South America)
Puerto Rican (Puerto Rico, Caribbean Island)
Salvadoran (El Salvador, Central America)
Surinamese (Suriname, South America)
Uruguayan (Uruguay, South America)
Venezuelan (Venezuela, South America)

simply mean those influences that came from the peoples and cultures of the many nations comprising Latin America. That's a lot of countries and a lot of diverse influences!

Latin American Cuisine

Latino cuisine is nearly as hard to define as "Latino." It's impossible to pin down because its array of culinary approaches varies as much as the region itself. Think about it. Latin America encompasses nineteen different Spanish-speaking nations. This region is enormous, stretching 7,000 (11,265.4 kil.) miles from the northwestern border of Mexico to the southern tip of Argentina.

Between those two points exists every climate and geographical feature you can imagine. Parts of the region's west coast form extreme desert regions. Places in northern Chile have not seen one drop of rain since the beginning of recorded history! The high valleys of the Andes are cool all year. Uruguay and Argentina boast some of the best, temperate farmlands in the world. Belize is second only to Australia for its *barrier reef*. Mexico has equal shares of deserts, mountains, *savannahs*, and swamps.

Now consider the fact that the food a country's inhabitants eat largely depends on its geography. Diverse lands equal diverse native foods. Each region has its own *indigenous* foods and its own culinary habits. On top of that, specific dishes have innumerable versions based on local likes and dislikes. And if you think the diverse regions of Mexico and Central and South America influenced each other's peoples and their eating habits, you're mistaken.

---

barrier reef: a coral reef parallel to the shore, separated from it by a lagoon.

savannahs: tropical or subtropical grasslands containing scattered trees and drought-resistant undergrowth.

indigenous: native to the area.

Prickly pear is a native fruit popular in some Hispanic countries.

Immigration: Creating Change

Beans are native to the Americas.

Historically, contact among neighboring geographical areas was infrequent and sporadic. Ground transportation throughout much of Latin America was limited by its harsh, untamed terrain. Only a generation ago, many roads were no more than rough mule trails twisting through dense rain forests and rugged mountain passes. Consequently, many regions—even those within one country—remained isolated, developing customs and cuisines uniquely their own.

Still, common threads did (and do) exist throughout the Americas. Common culinary building-blocks included corn, squash, and beans. Wheat and rice were not found in the Americas until the arrival of Europeans, but corn was ground into flour or meal, which, in turn, was used as the main ingredient in cornbreads (*arepas*), *tortillas*, and *tamales*, all staples of the *pre-Columbian*, native diet. Corn's importance in Latino cuisine cannot be overstated, then or now.

Then there's the bean, also a shared staple of Latin America. We're talking all kinds of beans: red ones, black ones, white ones, little ones, big ones, round ones, oval ones. Beans were cooked, then eaten whole or mashed into a paste and seasoned. Pairing beans with corn or corn products was a common dish of the Americas.

Now add exploration to the mix. When the Spaniards arrived in this part of the New World, they encountered many groups of native people: the Maya, Inca, Aztecs, and others. Native and immigrant factions impacted each other profoundly, and both were forever changed. (We'll examine how later in the chapter.) The point is that modern, Latin American cuisine evolved from many sources and cannot be defined by strictly one ethnicity; it is the result of blending many cultures and tastes over multiple generations.

Roots of Change

The history of Latino cuisine begins with native people: the Maya, Inca, and Aztecs. These three groups are the most famous pre-Columbian civilizations, but others existed: Araucanian Indians (Chile and Argentina), Caribes (Caribbean), Chavins (Peru), Patagones (tip of South America), Tainos (Caribbean, the first to encounter the Spanish), and Tarascan (*Mesoamerica*).

---

tortillas: very thin, circular flatbreads made with flour or ground corn.

tamales: food made of a cornmeal dough stuffed with meat or vegetables, then wrapped in a cornhusk and steamed; variations exist throughout Latin America.

pre-Columbian: before the arrival of Columbus.

Mesoamerica: region including parts of eastern and southern Mexico, Belize, Guatamala, Honduras, and Nicaragua.

Hot Potato

The standard, white potato originated in the high Andean valleys of South America, not in Ireland (or Idaho!) like many people think.

socialism: an economic and political system characterized by ownership of the means of production by the state—there is no private property.

self-sustaining: ability to support oneself.

ingenious: clever.

conquistadors: conquerors.

Many of these civilizations were actually more advanced than most European civilizations of the time. The Maya were among the first to live in cities. Pyramids and temples built by the Maya, Inca, and Aztecs rivaled those of ancient Egypt. Some groups practiced forms of *socialism*, used decimal-based computing methods, and even had mail delivery systems!

Skilled soldiers, warriors, diplomats, politicians, hunters, gatherers, fishermen, and farmers, these native peoples were *self-sustaining* and *ingenious*. For example, when beans and corn didn't grow well in the high valleys of the Andes, the Inca cultivated potatoes that did. Many indigenous people were also great strategists: on encountering enemies, Aztecs tried to persuade leaders to join their empire, rather than kill them or battle over their land. Because of such ingenuity, these civilizations thrived for centuries.

Spanish Conquest

Everything changed in Latin America in the fifteenth century. In 1492, Columbus arrived in Cuba, San Salvador (an Island in the Bahamas), and Haiti; in 1493–96, he came to Puerto Rico; in 1498–1500, Trinidad and Venezuela; in 1502–4, Martinique and Central America. He was followed in 1500 by the *conquistadors* who came to South America, Central America, and southern Mexico: Hernando Cortés in 1519 in Central Mexico; Pedro de Alvarado in the 1520s in Guatemala and El Salvador; Francisco Pizarro in 1532 in Peru.

The tomato is native to the Americas.

Immigration: Creating Change

autonomous: having the right or power of self-rule.

Roughly five hundred years ago, many conquistadors claimed lands for Spain, but contrary to popular legend, war and conquest were not the primary reasons the native empires fell. Natives lacked immunity to the new diseases—such as smallpox—imported by the Europeans. The two worlds simply collided—and the native Americans came out the worse.

Mixed Blood

In the years that followed, Spanish settlers encountered many different native peoples in the Americas—sometimes called collectively "Amerindians"—and eventually they intermarried and interbred with those they conquered. When you consider that the Spaniards themselves were a diverse group—there were five distinct *autonomous* regions in Spain at that time—plus they eventually also brought people from Africa as slaves, it's no wonder that the result is an ethnic group more diverse in physical appearance, traditions, and culture than any other in the world. (For example, some Latinos look white; others appear tan; still others have dark brown skin—and all are Latino.) Spaniards from all five regions in Spain—each with its own identity, dialect, and customs—settled in Mexico, Central America, and South America. So did some Africans. The different linguistic and cultural characteristics of each region (including culinary habits) blended with the existing melting pot of Amerindian languages and customs. And modern Latin America was born.

Myth Buster

Did Italians use tomatoes in 1492? No! The tomato was cultivated by American Aztecs—who called it *xitomatl*—and wasn't introduced to Europe until Columbus returned from his voyages in the late fifteenth century.

The Aztecs called tomatoes xitomatl.

Immigration: Creating Change

Europeans had never tasted chilies or corn before they came to the New World.

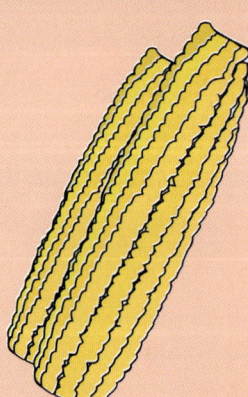

Royal Tastes

Hot chocolate—a bit different than our version—was a favorite beverage of pre-Columbian Aztec royalty.

Early Exchange

How did this marriage between the Americas and Europe impact traditional eating? Dramatically! Both sides of the Atlantic adopted culinary influences from the opposite shore.

When the Spanish anchored in "New World" waters, they encountered foods unlike any they'd seen in the "Old World." Chocolate, vanilla, chilies, sweet peppers, tomatoes, potatoes,

New World or Old World?

Many people of European descent speak of the Americas as the "New World," while Europe is referred to as the "Old World." But it's really all a question of point of view. For people who are native to the Americas, their own world is the familiar, "old" world, while Europe, the strange world across the ocean, seems like a "new" world.

peanuts, tobacco, and corn, corn, corn were just a few. None of these foods had previously touched the European palate.

In turn, local Amerindians—the Maya, Aztecs, Inca—tasted rice, olives, grapes, cheese, and meats like pork, beef, and chicken (brought by the Europeans) for the first time. Fifteenth-century Natives ate mostly vegetables, beans, and fruit, plus wild turkey, pheasants, venison, rabbits, and fish. They hadn't heard of domestic cows, pigs, and chickens yet, let alone dairy products.

The result? Trade was inevitable between these two groups—and they didn't just trade food products. The exchange of culinary uses and preparation methods also flourished. A cultural shift began, and European and American foods changed forever. Latino cuisine was off to a great start.

Latin Explosion

U.S. Latino populations as recorded by the U.S. Census:
1980: 14,608,673
1990: 22,354,059
2000: 35,300,000

Banana farmers in Mexico

The Impact of Immigration

Move ahead 250 years. After the United States gained independence in 1776, people from some of the Spanish colonies—mostly Mexico, Cuba, Puerto Rico, and Colombia—began moving north to seek a better life. The next two hundred years brought the Spanish-American War; the Cuban Revolution; bloody dictatorships in Central and South American countries; civil wars in Nicaragua, El Salvador, and Guatemala; and hundreds of other political upheavals from Mexico to Argentina. Latinos, looking for safety, stability, health, and prosperity, fled their countries of origin in record numbers.

Many of these immigrants poured into the United States, bringing with them the wonderful diversity that defines their culture. Puerto Ricans were the first big group of Latinos (excluding Mexicans) to arrive; they hit U.S. shores largely during the post–World War II era. Cubans, Dominicans, Colombians, and Costa Ricans began arriving in mass during the 1960s. The 1970s saw the advent of Salvadorans, Bolivians, Peruvians, and more.

The 1970s marked the beginning of a surge in Latino immigration that has not slowed down. Over the last three decades, the number of Latinos living in the United States has increased by more than 100 percent, although much of the increase was due to high birth rates within the population. In fact, according to the 2000 U.S. Census, 35.3 million Latinos now call the United States home. That number increased to 35.8 million just

Making "nopales" from prickly pear

Immigration: Creating Change

Latino Cuisine

A Latino street vendor sells tacos and other Hispanic foods.

Where Do Latinos Live in the United States?

The greatest concentration of Latinos belongs to the southwest; six of ten states reporting the most Latino residents live there. Appearing highest to lowest, these states include New Mexico (42 percent of the state's population), California (32 percent), Texas (32 percent), Arizona (25 percent), Nevada (19 percent), Colorado (17 percent). Other states with a high percentage of Latino residents include Florida (16 percent), New York (15 percent), New Jersey (13 percent), and Illinois (12 percent).

While most Latinos seem to gravitate to large cities (like Los Angeles, Chicago, and New York), Latinos are increasingly moving to medium- and small-sized cities (like Atlanta, Albuquerque, and Grand Rapids). Some even prefer rural farming areas.

(Source: U.S. Census Bureau)

I remember my first experience eating Mexican food as a child. One Sunday morning I returned from church to smell a new aroma in the house, wafting from the kitchen. It wasn't something familiar, like my grandmother's French Canadian breakfasts of baked beans with molasses, eggs, and homemade breads with country honey and butter. It wasn't my godmother's spicy pasta sauce with Italian sausage. The aroma was much stronger, hanging in the room like a string of Christmas lights. In the kitchen I found my mother cooking juicy red sausage. Slowly sizzling in the skillet, it was loose and rich. This was the source of the intriguing smell. Impulsively, I took a bit on a fork and blew on it to cool it down. When I put it in my mouth, there was an explosion of flavors, and then a quiet blast of heat. This was my first of many breakfasts of scrambled eggs, chorizo, corn tortillas, and hot chocolate. I was hooked.
—from the foreword of *The Border Cookbook*, by Cheryl Alters and Bill Jamison.

over the last four years (an increase of .5 million!), and it doesn't include Latin Americans living in Canada.

Officially edging out African Americans in the 2000 Census, Latinos are now the largest minority group in the United States. According to the U.S. Census Bureau, they represent a full 13 percent of the nation's population, and their numbers are expanding at a rate nearly *double* that of the general population. Two-thirds of these Latinos are Mexican in origin, while the remaining 12 million have their roots all over Latin America. Sixty percent, or roughly 21 million, were born in the United States.

Latin American people groups are infiltrating every geographical region of the United States. Latino influence is evident everywhere on the continent! How, then, can mainstream America—its culture, customs, and cuisines—*not* be influenced by such steady and significant growth? Latino culture—and cuisine—is bound to become part of the fabric of America—and we're a richer, more diverse nation for it.

Habla Español

arepas (ah-ray-pas): flat, cornmeal cakes originating in Colombia and Venezuela; generally flavored with cheese.

chorizo (choh-ree-soh): sausage

maiz (mah-ees): corn

tomate (toh-mah-tay): tomato

Latino Cuisine

2

Inception:
Reaching Regions
and Restaurants

Adelaida and Macario Cuellar immigrated to the United States from Mexico in the early 1900s. Like many Latinos crossing the southern border, the couple was looking for a better life in America. Willing to work hard to realize their dream, they started working a small farm in Kaufman County, Texas.

A Mexican American man sells nuts and spices outside his restaurant in Chimayo, New Mexico.

The physical work was never-ending, but money remained tight. So in 1926, Adelaida decided to open a little stand at the Kaufman County Fair to sell her homemade tamales and chili. She never dreamed her stand would draw the crowds it did. People who came to the fair devoured her cooking! Tamales were a hit.

The fair ended, but the demand for Adelaida's Mexican cooking did not. With the help of her twelve children, Adelaida Cuellar opened a small café. In 1940, five of her sons moved the small restaurant to Oak Lawn in Dallas, Texas. Using their mother's traditional recipes, El Chico was born, and the restaurant became a Dallas tradition. Today, nearly a hundred El Chico restaurants are doing business in Texas, Louisiana, Oklahoma, and throughout the south.

After a visit to California where she was exposed to the great tastes of Mexican cuisine, Marno McDermott, a University of Minnesota graduate, decided that such food and drink were simply too festive not to share. Why should the Southwest get all the fun? So Marno teamed up with former Green Bay Packer Max McGee, and they converted Max's Left Guard Bar into the first Chi-Chi's.

Amazingly, sales soared to $2 million the first year. True to McDermott's vision of spreading flavorful fun, the number of Chi-Chi's restaurants skyrocketed to ninety-two within the first five years, and revenues grew to nearly $100 million. Mexican food was a hit in the Midwest.

Millions of happy palates have savored Chi-Chi's signature dishes (such as the Outrageous Burrito, Presidente Enchiladas, Aztec Ribeye, and Mexican Fried Ice Cream) since that first

Chi-Chi's

Inception: Regions and Restaurants

Latino Cuisine

Hispanic food is popular today with almost all Americans.

restaurant made its debut in 1976. To that end, Chi-Chi's has been a true pioneer, introducing full-service Mexican American dining not only to the Midwest, but also to much of the Northeast. In 2004, after almost thirty years in business, the Chi-Chi's chain closed.

Two women; two restaurant chains; two very different tales. Adelaida Cuellar was a recent immigrant born of authentic Mexican blood. Kaufman County, Texas, had the good fortune of tasting tamales because of the family's financial need. Marno McDermott and Max McGee, on the other hand, were U.S. citizens from the Midwest. With names like McDermott and McGee, Latino cooking surely was not the norm in their households, but they recognized good food when they encountered it. Minnesota got to experience just how good simply because McDermott wanted to share some fun.

Authentic Latino cook. . .

Fun-loving, Midwestern *entrepreneur*. . .

Both introduced the tastes of Mexico to their respective regions.

entrepreneur: someone who organizes, manages, and assumes the risks of a business.

From Kitchen to Café

All across North America, a flavor revolution is redefining dining out. Much like other ethnic cuisines such as Italian, Asian, or French, Latino food has become a significant player in the restaurant scene. How exactly did Latino cuisine become so popular? The stories with which we opened this chapter illustrate the chronology perfectly.

Immigrants from south of our borders arrive in a new region of America (like the Cuellars). They cook as they always have, then share their dishes with others, either through casual friendship or formal business endeavors. Local people taste Latin American cooking, many for the first time. They love it, want more, and customer demand increases.

So the immigrants increase production, sell more, and open additional restaurants. This activity spreads the new cuisine into new areas, and more people taste the zesty fare. Add to that

> **Fun Fact**
>
> The legislature of the Lone Star State made chili the official dish of Texas.

the fact that Latin American food is largely fast and cheap—providing a filling, flavorful meal when you don't have much money or time to spend—and even greater numbers of Americans desire the cuisine. Production increases with demand, and the cycle continues.

Time goes by. The "new" foods gain popularity in a specific region. Maybe a friend or tourist visits from another part of the country and loves the flavors to which she's introduced (like McDermott, when she visited California). The visitor, much like an immigrant, brings recipes, ingredients, and/or preparation methods for the cuisine back to her area. A similar process begins, and Latino cuisine has suddenly spread nationwide.

Stirring the Competition

Next, competing restaurants enter the picture: steak houses, family restaurants, pancake houses, sandwich shops, burger joints, pizza places, and even establishments known for "fine dining." They witness the growth in popularity of Latino foods and, as wise businesses, seek a piece of the action. The adventurous (or greedy!) begin to add occasional Latino-influenced items—"specials"—to established menus, and observe how they sell.

If the new item is not a big seller, they drop it from the menu. No harm done. If it's a hit with customers, the item remains and additional Latino-influenced dishes likely appear. Now basic Latin American dishes reach mainstream America.

Take, for instance, IHOP (International House of

Cuban food is gaining popularity.

Latin American Items on Menus of Popular Chains

Applebee's: Chicken Quesadilla Grande, Fajitas con Sizzle, Fiesta Lime Chicken, Nachos Nuevos, Santa Fe Chicken Salad

Atlantic Bread Company: Cuban Pork Loin Sandwich

Beef O'Brady's: Cuban Sandwich

Bennigans: Caribbean Crab Cakes, Fajita Chicken Quesadillas, Southwest Sampler

Coyote Café: Ecuadorian Ceviche, Sopa de Habaña, Bisteak Sosa

Cheesecake Factory: Baja Chicken Tacos, Crispy Taquitos, Factory Burrito Grande, Factory Nachos, Quesadillas, Stuffed Chicken Tortilla, Sweet Corn Tamales

T.G.I. Friday's: Chargrilled Chicken or Beef Fajitas, Chicken Quesadillas, Tostado Nachos

Houlihan's: Anaheim Chicken and Carmelized Onion Quesadilla, Chipolte Chicken Nachos, Cubano Sandwich, Southwest Chicken Wrap, Sizzling Fajitas

IHOP (International House of Pancakes): Tex-Mex Omelette, Southwest Chicken Fajita Salad

Perkins: Bread Bowl Chili, Caribbean Chicken Salad, El Grande Omelette, Burrito, Quesadillas (three types), Sante Fe Fajita Chicken, Sante Fe Mini Chimi's

Pizza Hut: Fiesta Taco Pizza

Planet Hollywood: "High Plains Drifter" Beef Nachos, "Jurassic Park" Fajitas, Mexican Vegetable Enchiladas, Neve's Mexican Beef Taco Salad, Spicy Cuban Beef Sandwich, Spicy Cuban Beef Salad, "The Three Amigo's" VIP Platter

Red Lobster: Artichoke Lobster Dip with Tortilla Chips, Aztec Chicken, Fiesta Lobster Rolls

Pancakes). It's a *pancake* house, for goodness sake! Still, the family-dining giant offers a "Tex-Mex Omelette" featuring salsa among other ingredients mixed into a three-egg omelet. Mimi's Café, a chain of eighty-three cafés from Florida to Kansas to California popular for its classic American dishes, recently added a "Huevos con Tortillas" platter to its breakfast menu. The platter includes three scrambled eggs, cheddar cheese, green onions, sour cream, fresh salsa, avocado, black beans, and chipotle sauce served with warm tortillas.

As you can see, more and more non-Latino restaurants are delving into Latin American fare. They'd be foolish not to. According to the Food Service Research Institute, 11 percent of all items on chain-restaurant menus are now Mexican (an increase of about 25 percent since 1997). But what about the rest of Latin America: Cuba, Jamaica, Puerto Rico, Argentina, Chile, Peru, and others?

Collectively called "Latino" cuisine by the food-service industry (separate from Mexican), these ethnicities account for only one additional percent of all chain-menu items. Still, 18.7 percent of all chain restaurants (about one of every five) feature at least one non-Mexican, Latino item; 32.1 percent (or one in three) casual restaurant chains, the most frequented sit-down places among Americans, offer the same.

Excluding Mexican (the most popular by far), what are the leading Latino cuisines invading American chain restaurants? According to the Food Service Research Institute, Caribbean delights win by a landslide. The following regional foods are

A busy Cuban restaurant

A Puerto Rican restaurant in New York City

increasingly appearing at the likes of Planet Hollywood, TGI Fridays®, Red Lobster, and the Cheesecake Factory:

Caribbean (52 percent of all non-Mexican, Latino chain-menu items)

South American (five percent)

Cuban (three percent)

Central American and "other" (32 percent)

Immigration, a powerful driver of the ethnic foods explosion, has been strong from the Caribbean and Central and South America, especially in recent years. The U.S. Immigration and Naturalization Services (INS) reported that 10 percent of all immigrants over the last decade came from the Caribbean alone. Another five percent came from Central and South America. But Mexican cuisine remains the strongest player in Latino influence on American taste buds. Consider the success of sit-down restaurants like Casa Olé (forty-plus locations), Chevy's Fresh Mex (110+ locations in over seventeen states nationwide), and El Chico (100+ locations). Mexican food's popularity is hard to ignore.

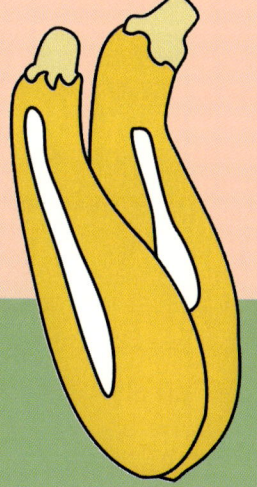

amigo (ah-mee-goh): friend

restaurante (rayst-ow-rahn-tay): restaurant

savor (sah-vore): flavor

Spanish Words Often Found on American Menus

adobo: marinade; sauce

boniato: a Latin tuber described as a white sweet potato

burro or burrito: flour tortilla rolled up around a warm filling, sometimes topped with a sauce or salsa; condiments remain on the outside. ("Ito" at the end of "burrito" simply implies something small; a burro is a large version of a burrito.)

carne: meat

cazuela: an earthenware casserole or pot

ceviche: shellfish or fish seasoned with and/or cooked only in citrus juices like lemon and lime, not heated; added ingredients vary

chili: (1) thick, stew-like dish made with ground meat, beans, tomatoes, and chili peppers ("con carne" simply means "with beef")

chili: (2) any of a variety of peppers (for example, ancho chilies or poblano chilies)

chimichurri: pesto-like, all-purpose herb sauce similar to a vinaigrette; usually made of parsley, cilantro, olive oil, vinegar, herbs, and spices

chipolte: a ripened, smoked jalapeño

chupe: chowder

enchiladas: rolled tortillas stuffed with meat or cheese filling, served with chili sauce

fajitas: grilled fare wrapped in warm, flour tortillas

guava: yellow-skinned fruit of a tropical American tree; used primarily for jellies

huevos: eggs

nachos: tortilla chips served with melted cheese and other toppings

pollo: chicken

quesadilla: meat or veggies and cheese sandwiched between two, flat flour tortillas, then lightly fried until slightly crisp on both sides; often cut like a pizza and usually served with salsa, shredded lettuce, and sour cream on the side

queso: cheese

quinoa: herb seed used much like a grain

salsa: technically any sauce, but known widely as a seasoned, diced-tomato sauce made with other fresh, raw ingredients; served cold as a condiment or with tortilla chips

sofrito: a mixture of onions, peppers, garlic, herbs, and spices; the specific blend depends on country of origin and individual chefs; the base of many Latin dishes

sopa: soup

tacos: meat, beans, cheese and/or rice in a hard or soft, corn or flour tortilla, but more familiarly served in a crisp, corn-tortilla shell; add-ons (like lettuce) and condiments (like salsa) go on the inside with the filling

tamale: cornmeal dough stuffed with meat or vegetables, then wrapped in a cornhusk and steamed; variations exist throughout Latin America

tomatillos: green fruit often mistaken for green tomatoes

tortilla: very thin, circular flatbread made with flour or ground corn

yucca: sweet, but starchy, root vegetable

Latino Cuisine

3

Innovation: "Fusing" Foods

Soy sauce mixed with mango juice? Bananas on fish served in half of a coconut? Avocado egg rolls?

Do these combinations seem "loco" to you? They might sound crazy, but each one is an actual restaurant item. Winds of change are definitely on the horizon.

Many Mexican restaurants are thriving businesses.

The Mexican food craze that began thirty years ago shows no sign of abating. In the 1970s, when Mexican restaurants started appearing all over the United States, dishes like burritos and tacos began showing up on mainstream menus. Then came the "Tex-Mex" craze, adding spicy Southwest flavors, fajitas, and tapas to the mix. By the '90s, authentic Mexican food made with fresh ingredients had become "in demand." It still is.

But Americans are a savvy and insatiable group. Simply "Mexican" doesn't cut it any more. Through greater travel to Latin America and more exposure to the unique cuisines of its many countries via the media and other sources, diners have become familiar with a much wider spectrum of Latin foods, flavors, and cooking methods.

Innovation: "Fusing" Foods

I can't remember a time when food wasn't the most important thing in my life. And I can't remember a time when the kitchen wasn't my favorite place to be. Especially in my grandmother's house, where I had been sent to live at a very early age. . . . A child in love with food could have asked no more.

The cuisine of my childhood was very eclectic. My grandmother's influences were those of her native Chile—heavily Spanish—with touches of her German background. Of course, she loved seafood, the predominant food in Chile, a long coastal country. My mother's parents were Italian, so the Italian influence was there, though it was not as strong as their adopted country, Peru. Peruvian cuisine reflects the country's mixture of cultures: those of the Spanish, the native Quechua Indians, and black Africans, who were brought over as slaves by Spanish colonials. The kitchen in my grandmother's house was an even greater cultural melting pot as a result of the kitchen helpers who worked for my mother and grandmother. Around great feast days extra help was needed, and women from all over South America—including Bolivia and Brazil—would be brought in, as well as Peruvian Indian women. My kitchen education was a United Nations of cultural influence.

—Felipe Rojas-Lombardi, chef and owner of the Ballroom Restaurant in New York (from the introduction in his book *The Art of South American Cooking*)

Fast Facts

- Twenty-four Latin Americans currently serve in the U.S. Congress.
- Arturo Manheim, owner of the Anaheim Angels, is the first Latino to own a major-league franchise.
- Soccer (called football in Latin American countries) has replaced baseball as the number-one youth sport.

Watered-down Americanized versions are out. Authenticity is in. Restaurant patrons and home cooks alike are continually seeking new adventures in taste. It's now chic to explore those little Caribbean, Ecuadorian, Brazilian, or Peruvian storefront restaurants.

Combine these trends with the fact that the Latino population continues to grow in number and spending power faster than any other group. Suddenly the lightbulb goes off. Mainstream America is becoming more and more Latin American by the decade! And, as with many second- and third-generation ethnic groups, settled Latinos are increasingly open to venturing beyond traditional tastes to experience—and even adopt—bold flavors of other Latin countries.

To that end, a new breed of Latin American restaurant is focusing on regional recipes while trying to broaden its menus to include dishes from more than one country. We've seen

A Cuban sandwich

Innovation: "Fusing" Foods

renowned American chefs traveling through Mexico and Central and South America to document on TV multiple, regional cuisines they then feature in their restaurants. Nacional 27, a Chicago-based restaurant, takes its name from the twenty-seven Latino countries shaping its menu.

Additionally, some chefs are beginning to explore blending ethnicities. Take Avacado Eggrolls, TexMex Eggrolls, and Chino-Latino Steak for instance. The Cheesecake Factory now offers all three items, obvious blends of Asian and Latin fare. Pizza Hut's "Fiesta Taco Pizza" is clearly merging traditional Italian with Latino foods. Avocado pastas, Southwestern salads, and garlic potatoes are just a few of the many "fusion" creations appearing all across the nation. If only our diplomats could come together so easily and so well!

Nuevo Latino

Nuevo Latino is the rage in fine-dining. A recent cooking trend expected to endure, its earlier names included "New Caribbean," "New Floridian," "Floribbean," and even "New World" cuisine. This approach combines the food cultures of the Latin American mainland and the Caribbean by blending old and new cooking styles, flavors, and ingredients (for example, corn and plantains [a banana-like fruit], or chilies and tropical fruits). The main influences for Nuevo Latino cuisine come from Cuba and Puerto Rico, with others emerging from Peru and Brazil.

"If I had to pick one current food fad I believe has a chance of becoming an enduring American genre, it would most certainly be Nuevo Latino cuisine," attests John Mariana of *Wine Spectator* magazine. The reviews are in. Food columnists nationwide echo his sentiments.

Ironically, but not surprisingly, the first Nuevo Latino restaurants were run by non-Latinos who weren't tied to specific cooking traditions. They simply used whatever was available, mixing unheard-of combinations of spices, herbs, and regional foods, regardless of ethnicity. But Cuban American Douglas Rodriguez was the one who dramatically launched this fusion cuisine when he opened Yuca in Miami and later Patria in New York. Rodriguez first offered such creations as guava-basted barbeque ribs and plantain-crusted mahi-mahi. But he broke all the rules at Patria, mixing Guatamalan, Brazilian, Peruvian, and Cuban ingredients (such as yucca, boniato, chilies, black beans, guava, and bananas) into highly colorful, spicy creations. For example, his "Caribbean Bouillabaisse" is a sofrito- and cilantro-spiced soup of shrimp, scallops, mussels, and clams served in an elegant cazuela. In another dish, plantain chips tower over a grouper ceviche artistically arranged in a coconut half-shell that's set in a delicate wine glass.

"Douglas was using Latin-American ingredients in ways no one had ever imagined," commented *Gourmet* magazine editor-in-chief Ruth Reichl. (His latest experiment? He likes to fold Kikkoman Soy Sauce in with citrus juices, inviting yet another ethnicity into his kitchen.) Now you see dishes Rodriguez invented everywhere. Chefs he trained have fanned out along the East Coast where they've had a big impact. Say goodbye to ketchuppy tacos and gloppy burritos; world-class Nuevo Latino chefs are redefining Latin American food.

> **Douglas Rodriguez**
>
> Douglas Rodriguez, one of America's most honored chefs, is considered the "*papi grande*," the "big daddy," the inventor of Nuevo Latino cuisine.

Moving On

Clearly, the Latin Explosion of the last few centuries has influenced our taste buds irreversibly. Americans love Latino food; the fast-food market is no exception. In the next chapter we'll take a look.

Habla Español

loco (loh-koh): crazy

fiesta (fee-ace-tah): party, festival, celebration

gringo (green-go): a white person from the United States

nuevo (noo-ae-voh): new or again

Latino Cuisine

4

Ignition:
Fiery Fast Foods

"You can't grow your business if your menu is not exciting people," says David Sonzongi, vice-president of culinary services at Bennigans®. "You really do have to push the envelope and develop new products." In the last chapter we saw that that philosophy was certainly wise—and profitable—for sit-down restaurants trying Hispanic cuisine, but what about fast food?

Latino Cuisine

Latino fast food is enjoyed by many Americans.

executives: people in charge of running a company.

Here's a fast-food quiz: What do Boston Market, Burger King, Chik-fil-a, Jack in the Box, McDonald's, Popeye's, Quizno's, Schlotzsky's, Sonic Drive-In, Subway, and Wendy's have in common? Apparently they all agree with Sonzongi; they've all caught the Latino craze.

The same motive that's been driving sit-down restaurants to add Latin dishes to their menus is also influencing fast-food *executives*: profit. The Latino population is the fastest growing portion of the U.S. population. You can't deny the census. (By 2020, nearly 60 million Latinos will call the United States home.) As the popularity of Latin American flavors expands among the Latin American community, an increasing segment of the general population will be hungering for them, too.

Consumption of Mexican food among non-Latino baby-boomers rose 84 percent between 1986 and 1995. Add to that

Fresh Ideas in Fast Fare

A sampling of Latino dishes offered at non-Latino fast-food chains

Boston Market:	Grilled Mango Chicken, Southwest Chicken Salad
Burger King:	Santa Fe Fire-Grilled Chicken Baguette
Chick-fil-a:	Spicy Chicken Cool Wrap, Caesar Wrap
Jack in the Box:	Chicken Fajita Pita, Southwest Chicken Salad, Monster Taco
McDonald's:	Sausage Burrito, Fiesta Salad
Popeye's:	Red Beans and Rice
Quizno's:	Chili, Three Santa Fe Sandwiches, Turkey Bacon Guacamole Sandwich (all sandwiches can be on "flatbread")
Schlotzsky's:	Salsa Chicken with Cheddar on Sourdough Bread
Sonic Drive-In:	Chicken Wrap, Breakfast Burrito
Subway:	Southwest Turkey Bacon Sub, Chicken Bacon Ranch Wrap
Wendy's:	Taco Supreme Salad

Latino Cuisine

Latin American foods are a part of young adult life.

the fact that the fast-paced American lifestyle shows no sign of slowing, and you've got yourself a recipe for guaranteed success: America's love affair with Latino flavors plus busy people. Mexican fast-food is hot!

Enter McDonald's, Quiznos, Jack in the Box, and the rest. They're no fools. The Latino explosion is here; non-Latinos love the food, too; and traditional fast-food fare is old news. These companies' executives know that many on-the-go people are looking for alternatives to burgers and sandwiches.

Suddenly tortillas are everywhere, but the name has changed to "wraps." "Southwest" and "Sante Fe" are common adjectives for new salads and chicken sandwiches. Burritos line up right next to Egg McMuffins® on breakfast menus.

But were any of the traditional, fast-food giants the first to dish up Latin American quick-service? No. "Who was?" you might be wondering. To answer that, let's go back to the years immediately following World War II.

Glen Bell was twenty-three years old when he left the Marine Corps in 1946. He came home from war to his sleepy hometown of San Bernardino, California, with an idea. Many local, recreational activities had disappeared during wartime years as people and supplies were rerouted to the war effort. Why not start a business that filled the void?

Mr. Bell's first idea was a miniature golf course, but the start-up costs were too expensive. So he went to work on something more suited to his wallet: a hot dog stand. Bell's Drive-In was a strictly take-out business that Glen learned to run as he went along.

In 1952, he sold that stand and began work on an improved version. This time, the menu would offer both hot dogs and hamburgers. (As he was building this second stand, the McDonald brothers were starting their first restaurant, also in San Bernardino. We all know what happened to them!) The second stand, too, was a success, but Mr. Bell became increasingly restless. He wanted to try new ideas for menu items. Tacos came to mind.

As an avid Mexican take-out customer, Glen Bell knew all too well the problems of ordering tacos "to go" from full-service restaurants. Frankly, it was a pain. "If you wanted

Taco Bell is a favorite fast-food restaurant.

a dozen, you were in for a wait," he recalls. There had to be something someone could do to quicken taco preparation. Glen wanted to be that someone, and he was determined to develop that something.

Research began. Mr. Bell learned as much as he could about taco shells and filling, while simultaneously searching for a good location to open his next stand. Still experimenting with mass taco preparation, Glen opened the new stand on a busy San Bernardino street near a Mexican neighborhood. He began with selling various hot dogs, including a chili dog. Once satisfied with his taco-making process, he decided to add the nineteen-cent treats to his menu, selling them from a little window off the side of his stand. The tacos were an instant hit. Glen Bell had firmly planted the roots of Taco Bell, which he initially called Taco Tias.

Taco Bell's founder began to focus on just tacos and was soon ready to open a second location. He settled on the town of Barstow even though it was a bit far away. Busy with the San Bernardino location, he left day-to-day operations of the new site up to a man named Ed Hackbarth. Hackbarth later built his own stand (1964) as the founder of Del Taco, a similar chain.

Today there are over 7,000 Taco Bells and over 400 Del Tacos across the nation. Clearly these two fast-food chains were the first to offer Latin American cuisine in the quick-service industry, and their entire menus were devoted to it! Adding one or two token dishes decades later—like the fast-food restaurants with which we opened the chapter—hardly seems significant. Yet American appetites don't seem to care. Sales are soaring in both places.

Latin American Fast-Food Restaurants

Yes, Taco Bell and Del Taco were the first in Mexican fast-food, and they're still the biggest. Yet for years, business was just stable, not rapidly rising. The late 1970s and '80s actually saw a lull in the marketplace. Then the Latino cuisine craze of the late twentieth century hit. Sales jumped, and the king and queen of quick-service Latin-based food soon had genuine competition.

Several new, strictly Latino quick-service chains opened, and consumers responded with their wallets. Cost-conscious families and students loved the prices; bored fast-food frequenters loved their new choices. Even famous athletes—basketball players with the Utah Jazz—were spotted in at least one newcomer: Café Rio. The new chains were making a splash in the calm waters of Mexican quick-service.

Joining Enemy Camps

Mexican quick-service restaurants have been around as long as McDonald's, and if you count that first little tamale stand we told you about

Who are these newcomers? What other fast-food chains boast strictly Latin American cuisine? Here are the most popular:

Baja Fresh (established 1990; 288+ locations)

Chipotle (established 1993; 40+ locations)

El Pollo Loco (established 1975; 300+ locations)

Qdoba Mexican Grill (established 1995; 100+ locations)

Taco John's (established 1969; 400+ locations)

Note how many of these chains entered the race as recently as 1990 or later. Look how quickly they've spread. Such success is yet another sign of growing Latino influence on American cuisine.

in the last chapter, a lot longer. Yet their popularity and success remain largely understated in the mainstream consciousness, at least by McDonald's standard. Consequently you might think chains like Taco Bell don't concern traditional, fast-food empires like McDonald's, Burger King, or Wendy's.

In fact, however, three burger giants were so concerned about the competition, their respective corporations each invested in a Latino fast-food establishment of its own: Wendy's purchased Baja Fresh in 2002, McDonald's bought Chipotle, and Jack in the Box owns Qdoba Mexican Grill. Even Taco Bell is part of the corporation that owns Pizza Hut and KFC. Adding a menu item simply isn't enough anymore, and these expansions answer concerns about tapping the lucrative, Mexican fast-food market, the only current growth area in the industry.

Changes

The big names in taco take-out and burgers are now encountering a third entrant to the Mexican quick-service game. Entirely new eateries are reinventing the genre. Places like Café Rio, Rubio's Baja Grill, Barbacoa, La Salsa, and Guru's are mixing the fast-food mentality with authentic flavor from south of the border, but Taco Bell they're not. Anything suggesting prepackaged foods, such as sauce packets or bags of tortilla chips, is out. Not one of these chains offers a drive-thru, and none serves a hard-shell taco.

The formula, though, is much the same as the big guys': basic common ingredients—all of which are used for a variety of dishes—set up assembly-line fashion for rapid food production. Here's how it works.

The company decides on its staples: tortillas, beans, chicken and beef mixtures, rice, shredded cheeses, salsas, hot sauces, seasonings, tomatoes, and lettuce, for example. To make a burrito, workers wrap a soft, flour tortilla around the meat, beans, and cheese, then put the lettuce on the side. If those same workers leave that tortilla unrolled (flat), pile the lettuce on top, and add chicken, tomatoes, and cheese, then

organic: grown naturally, without the use of pesticides and chemicals.

saturated: full; cannot hold anymore.

debuted: started; appeared.

voila!—they've made a Mexican salad from the same assembly line. Talk about efficiency! The staples determine the menu.

With an ordering counter, large overhanging menu, and separate condiment and drink stations, these newcomers fit right into to the fast-food genre, but don't be fooled. Many make their own tortillas fresh each day; some offer a host of flavors in their sauces; others use only the freshest, even *organic*, ingredients. A few even sell additional ethnic cuisines like teriyaki chicken rice and blackened halibut salad (for example, Guru's).

Clearly Mexican fast food is changing. The demand for authentic, regional flavors and the fusion of ethnicities we examined in the fine-dining industry are beginning to seep into a new breed of Latin-inspired fast-food chains. Watch out, Taco Bell. The bar for convenient Latino food is rising.

Survival

Let's be honest; the fast-food market is *saturated*, and the Latin American segment is increasingly no exception. Three of the most popular chains *debuted* just in the last decade. How can any player in this business continue to attract customers? One word: trends.

Studying what's popular, not only in the restaurant industry, but also in fine dining, home groceries, regional spending, and international markets is critical. Staying ahead of crazes, or at least responding to them, can make or break any establishment. Hot sauce is what's hot at the beginning of the twenty-first century, particularly in the South. (We'll examine sauces in chapter 5.)

According to Packaged Facts, a market research firm, the following figures indicate the geographic locations of consumers who buy hot sauces:

The South: bought 41 percent of all hot sauces sold nationwide

The West: bought 25 percent of all hot sauces sold nationwide

The Midwest: bought 22 percent of hot sauces sold nationwide

The Northeast: bought 12 percent of hot sauces sold nationwide.

Chilies and garlic—two important Latino ingredients

market niche: *a particular corner of a market.*

What should a company like Taco Bell do in response to this trend? Add menu items? Change their recipes? Stay the same? Initially, they need to take a hard look at themselves.

Remember those first chili dogs Glen Bell sold? Well, the sauce for the chili on those dogs became Taco Bell's signature taco sauce. Over the years, the company wisely added mild, hot, and fiery versions—one of the few restaurants that did—so they were prepared years ahead of the "hot sauces" craze. Other chains were not, however, and they're quickly scrambling to add a variety of the flaming concoctions to their menus.

The trick is coupling honest self-evaluation with flexibility: being willing to bend with the times if need be. In Taco Bell's case, after examining their "hot sauce" status, they realized they didn't need to adjust much. Other chains weren't so lucky. See if you notice any fiery additions at your favorite restaurant. Spot the trend!

Sometimes companies will try to develop a *market niche* instead of spotting trends. For instance, if yours is the only restaurant in town that offers ten kinds of chili, then you probably don't have to worry about hot sauces. If rice and beans draws your crowds, then the whole-grain movement in hoagie rolls won't affect you. Or if you're famous for chicken, pizza, or soup, adding flavored tortillas (another current trend) is almost irrelevant. Obviously, the ideal strategy is to create a niche that meets a lasting trend.

Moving On

Mexican fast food is currently the only Latin American cuisine widely available in quick-service foods. As we read in the last chapter, other culinary practices from south of our borders are impacting the sit-down restaurant niche, so fast food can't be far behind. Caribbean, Puerto Rican, Cuban, and other Latino cuisines will surely be making their marks in upcoming years. They're scarce now but not for long.

In the meantime, thirst-quenching delights from all of Latin America remain a constant import. Their influence has been huge on what we drink. Let's take a look at Latino impact on the beverage industry.

Habla Español

taco (tah-coh): spicy beef filling (usually topped with shredded cheese and salsa) that's rolled (soft taco) or stuffed (hard taco) into a tortilla shell (corn or flour). Condiments are on the inside of the shell.

burrito (boo-ree-toh): spicy bean-paste or meat filling and rice (usually topped with shredded cheese) rolled in a soft, flour tortilla. (Add-ons such as salsa, shredded lettuce and sour cream remain on the outside of the wrap.)

chipótle (chee-poh-tlay): a ripened, smoked jalapeño

5

Inundation: Broadening the Beverage World

I can't wait to set up! Becky thinks as she bounds down the steps. Her mom is having a huge yard sale, and Becky and her friends are manning a lemonade stand.

"Isn't it a bit early for lemonade?" her mom responds mid-yawn, stirring her morning coffee. "Why don't you wait at least until seven?"

Fascinating Fact

Europeans first dubbed lemons "golden apples."

Lemons are among the many fruits native to the Americas.

In summertime Americana, yard sales and lemonade stands sprout like dandelions as soon as crocuses bloom. Weekend mornings are greeted by exhausted parents nursing coffee mugs and frantic kids hocking sticky cups of lemonade to any who happen by.

American artist Norman Rockwell painted illustrations of "the lemonade stand"; radio host Garrison Keillor told stories about coffee; Southern belles sip both on shady porches, while countless ads romanticize each drink. How much more American can you get?

Yet we've been deceived. Many Americans don't realize that both lemonade and coffee have much more in common than just being popular beverages; each has its roots in Latin American soil. Technically, lemonade and coffee are imports!

Lemon Lore

Let's start with lemonade. A favorite drink of the Caribbean Islands is a mixture of lemon (or lime) juice, sugar, and water: in essence, lemonade. The Caribs (a group of people actually native to South America who settled on the islands, and also the group after which the islands are named) drank it long before Christopher Columbus arrived on their shores. That means they were drinking it long before we ever got here.

Think about it. What happens when you start with a hot

Inundation: Broadening the Beverage World

Lemonade, an all-American favorite, has its roots in Latin America.

climate with indigenous citrus fruit and add a clever, thirsty people? Limeade and lemonade! It makes sense, doesn't it? Limes, lemons, and sugarcane were (and are) plentiful in that region. The juicy citrus fruit was naturally flavorful but intense. Water was necessary to dilute the intensity; sugar countered the pucker-factor. The people drank their concoction by the gallons.

When explorers reached our southern shores after Columbus's trips to Cuba, Haiti, and Puerto Rico, they brought with them culinary habits learned on those first trips. Making and drinking lemonade was one of them. The beverage is as old as our country, and its ingredients don't need to be imported.

Today, almost every major bottling company has its own brand of ready-to-drink lemonade. Minute Maid® (the Coca-Cola Company), Snapple® (Snapple Beverage Corporation), and Tropicana® (the PepsiCo Company) are just a few. Country Time®, Crystal Light®, and Lipton® each have powdered versions anyone can mix at home. (Kool-Aid®—with its smiling pitcher—was one of the first to explore the powdered concept.) Lemonade is here to stay.

Why was this simple drink so able to withstand the test of time? It's easy to make, and it quenches great thirst, some think even better than water. No wonder it's so popular!

Coffee

In the 1720s, a young French naval officer, Gabriel Mathieu de Clieu, stepped off his vessel onto the shores of Martinique in the Caribbean carrying but a single tree

Coffee Crazies

- Europeans initially dubbed coffee "Arabian Wine."
- Bach wrote an entire cantata to coffee.
- Seventeenth-century European pharmacies first sold coffee as a medical remedy.
- Legend has is that coffee's caffeine effect was first discovered by a shepherd who noticed his flock got rather agitated and excitable after eating berries off low branches of small coffee trees.

seedling. Tradition claims that he kept the plant alive over the long voyage using part of his own meager water ration. Whether or not his sacrifice is true, that little tree became the ancestor of most of the billions of coffee trees now growing in Latin America.

Before the eighteenth century, coffee trees did not grow at all in Latin America. In fact, they're only indigenous to Africa and the Arabian Peninsula. So why are we including it in our discussion on Latino influences on American foods? Well, it's what Latin America did with that first twig that makes the difference. From one plant, Central and South America grew into the world's foremost coffee producers, an honor they still hold.

How did one small tree lead to such a distinction? In one word: flavor. Beans from trees grown in Central and South

Much of the world's coffee is grown in Central and South America.

"Fresh" Coffee, Anyone?

The practice of filtering coffee through cloth originated in Europe in the 1700s when someone poured hot water through a coffee-ground-filled sock. The new method of keeping grinds out of the pot—while allowing flavor in—was a hit. In many parts of the world today, coffee connoisseurs still use old socks to brew coffee.

America—as opposed to Africa and Indonesia—are generally light- to medium-bodied with clean, lively flavors. Compare that with the heavy, earthy tastes of Indonesian coffee or the complex, often spice-like flavors of African coffees and you soon understand the popularity of Latino coffee. Coffee quickly became the Americas' prime export.

Latin America is the land of coffee. The entire region is hugely dependent on its coffee crop. Local people drink coffee at every meal, even between meals, except in the southernmost countries. A Colombian coffee-drinker could commonly have a cup of coffee as soon as he wakes in the morning and keep drinking it throughout the whole day. In some rural areas, locals consider fifteen or even twenty cups daily a moderate habit.

Because coffee is so popular, "coffee breaks" are rare in many Latin American offices; the breaks would have to occur every ten minutes, and no work could ever get done. Instead, a person circulates among work areas, dispensing *tintos*, a strong Latino coffee

Coffee—or café—is a favorite Latino beverage.

made by placing ground coffee in a cone-shaped, cloth bag and pouring boiling water through it. It's quite strong, hence its name. (*Tintos* comes from the word *tinta*, which means ink.)

Obviously coffee has become an important part of Latino culture. It can also be a source of regional pride. For example, a Peruvian coffee-grower wouldn't dream of saying a good word about Brazilian coffee. And if you're Colombian, chances are you'd look down on any coffee that didn't come from your home region, even other Colombian ones.

Considering the strength of the average brew in Latin America and the degree of coffee-patriotism there, it's not surprising that most coffee-growing countries despise America's instant coffee. First of all, it's American. Second, most Latinos think it's flavorless. In fact, in Peru one brand (Nescafé®) was nicknamed "no es café" which means "it is not coffee"!

Inundation: Broadening the Beverage World

Latino Cuisine

Coffee beans

The Latinos who immigrated here over the last two centuries came from this robust coffee culture. These immigrants were used to full-bodied, fresh-brewed essences, not America's instant "brown water." Their kind of coffee was the only kind of coffee they wanted to make, buy, or sell. And just as we were influenced by their foods and cooking methods, we, too, shifted our coffee preferences in favor of a richer cup of java.

It's no coincidence, then, that increased interest in "good" coffee corresponds to the Latino explosion of the late twentieth century. Over the last thirty years, the demand for rich, authentic "single origin" (not a blend) coffees has skyrocketed, particularly in urban settings where Latino populations are densest. In response, chains like Starbucks® and the Coffee Beanery® sprung up in the 1970s, and java hasn't been the same since.

Let's look at these two chains. Both are in malls, shopping centers, and airports across the world. The Coffee Beanery® regularly lists such coffees as Colombian Supremo, Costa Rican Terrazu, Jamaican Blue Mountain, Costa Rican Minita, Mexican Aztec Pluma, Guatemalan Finca Dos Marias, Nicaraguan Segovai, and Guatemalan Huehuetenango on their coffee menu. Latin American beans outnumber African offerings by three times. How about Starbucks®? Latino coffees are the clear favorite there, too. With flavorful beans like Bella Vista FW Tres Rios®, Costa Rica, Brazil Ipanema Bourbon™, Colombia Nariño Supremo, Shade Grown Mexico, and Panama La Florentina, it's not surprising that the company has grown to over 7,500 locations worldwide.

Grocery stores now carry Costa Rican, Guatemalan, Mexican, Peruvian, Panamanian, and Colombian coffee beans right next to jars of Maxwell House® and Taster's Choice®. Convenience stores like WaWa® offer many international brands. (Gone are the "one-pot-on-a-warmer" days.) Plus local beaneries are popping up all over the country as consumers demand more authentic sipping experiences.

To take authenticity one step further, the truly hardcore coffee lovers now roast beans right at home. People buy beans raw, in bulk, or direct from importers and then roast them on their own home-roasting equipment. (At one time, simply grinding your own beans was extreme!) The home-coffee market is soaring.

Clearly, America's coffee habit has changed forever. We now drink a full-bodied cup of coffee closer to the "ink" of its adopted homeland. With the help of our Latino friends and their drive for authentic "café," many of us are experiencing our first real cup of coffee!

Habla Español

café (cah-fay): coffee

por ejemplo (pore ae-hame-ploh): for example

limón (lee-mone): lemon

taza (tah-sah): cup

Inundation: Broadening the Beverage World

Latino Cuisine

Infiltration: Alluring Alcohol

One of my favorite memories as a child was going on vacation with my dad's family. My uncles, their families, and my dad, mom, and brother—all of us—would share a tacky, enormous rental for one glorious week at the shore every July. It was heaven: eleven kids, all within five years of age, under the same roof, just a walking path away from sand castles and surf. Simply paradise.

distillation: the process of extracting the essence from something.

Burying bodies in the sand, making bathtubs by the tide, skimming, surfing, beach games, finding shells and sand dollars filled our days, but perhaps my fondest memory was of my mom. Yeah, my mom. Every day at 5:00 (cocktail hour) she would pull out the blender and make us kids the most glorious, frosty, yellow-green drinks I ever tasted.

With the care of a glassblower, she'd pour each ration into a "grown-up" glass and top it with a paper umbrella or a plastic sword stuck through a lime wedge. We thought we were royalty, grown-up royalty at that, and with one sip, any sunburn or jellyfish stings melted with the crushed ice.

What I didn't realize then was that Mom was making margaritas for us. Of course they were alcohol free, but we didn't know the difference. We'd sit around the table with our straws and umbrellas, pretending we were pirates stranded on a tropical island. We'd drink, act like drunken buccaneers, draw our plastic swords, drink again, then laugh until we cried.

—Maggie Donaldson, American college student

Latino drinks are popular across America.

While coffee is its most famous drink, Latin America has also developed a wide variety of alcoholic beverages. They range from excellent to quite dreadful. The native peoples of the region (the Maya, Inca, and Aztec) didn't originally contribute much in this area of consumption, but when the Spaniards showed up bringing grapes and **distillation** techniques, the situation rapidly and drastically changed. Today Latin America has a long list of native drinks, some of which find favor all over the world.

Frozen strawberry daiquiri

Infiltration: Alluring Alcohol

ferment: *to cause the breakdown of a compound.*

Tequila is probably Mexico's best-known "spirit." It's made from the starchy root of an indigenous plant called *agave azul tequilana*, hence the name. The roots are ground up, mixed with water, allowed to *ferment*, then distilled twice. The flavor is actually mild compared to whiskey, and its alcohol content is no stronger.

Nationals often drink tequila straight, but it's the cocktail to which it is added that's served millions of times a year across the nation. This drink took the casual sit-down restaurants by storm. What cocktail is it? The margarita.

You probably can't find a casual eatery that doesn't serve one. Red Lobster offers its Classic Margarita; Applebee's, the Perfect Margarita; Outback Steakhouse calls its version the Pacific Rim Rita. And, true to the insatiable American need for choices, margaritas now come in every fruit flavor imaginable: strawberry, peach, coconut—you name it. Latin Americans originally made it with lime juice.

Margarita

The margarita also imported creative ways of serving a beverage. A server moistens the rim of a wide glass and presses it lightly into coarse salt—so that the salt sticks to the rim—before pouring the drink into the glass. This tradition probably grew out of the manner in which Mexicans drink straight tequila.

In that case, the salt is placed "on-the-side" on a separate saucer with a wedge of lime. The drinker puts a pinch of salt on the back of his hand, tosses the salt into his mouth, drinks the tequila, then picks up the lime and sucks on it. The idea for using salt with both tequila and margaritas is to combine contrasting flavors at one time.

Cinco de Mayo (seen-coh day my-oh), the fifth of May, commemorates Mexico's independence from French rule much the same way as July Fourth celebrates the United States' independence from Britain. On May 5, 1862, the Mexicans defeated the French (under Napoleon) at the city of Puebla. (Independence from Spain is celebrated separately in September.) You might say that Cinco de Mayo is as important to Mexican Americans as St. Patrick's Day is to Irish Americans. And just like everyone is Irish on St. Patty's Day, even the most traditional Americans seem to turn Mexican on May fifth.

To fully comprehend just how mainstream the margarita has become, most people in the United States and Canada know to indicate "salt" or "no salt" when ordering. And lest you think all the fun surrounding this drink overlooks kids, "virgin" versions of the cocktail are also popular. ("Virgin," when added before a drink name, simply means no alcohol.)

How has the margarita impacted America cuisine? It's become *the* drink of our warm, coastal communities. Jimmy Buffet, a confessed beach bum, islander, and American singer-songwriter, topped the charts with his song *Margaritaville*. Grocery stores and warehouses like Sam's Club® and Costco® carry ready-made margarita mixes, particularly in the summer months. Additionally, special margarita glasses are everywhere. From fine glassware in better department stores to plastic versions at Walmart®, they crowd out other items on store shelves around the end of April and beginning of May.

Hispanic beverages

Why May? Because Cinco de Mayo is approaching (literally, five of May, Mexico's Independence Day). Cinco de Mayo parties have become almost as popular as July Fourth picnics for Mexican and non-Mexican Americans alike, and the drink of choice is the tequila-based margarita.

What about the rest of Latin America? Is Mexico's tequila the only "firewater" influencing American habits? Absolutely not. Rum has been equally influential.

In many parts of Latin America, the "wine of the country" is rum. The Caribbean gets credit for the origin of this powerful drink, and as was the case with lemonade, the region offers everything you need to distill it: sugarcane. Today, Americans use it in everything from *marinades* to shot glasses.

Rum, when used in cooking, adds flavor without any alcoholic effect. As the rum is heated, all but a very slight trace of the alcohol evaporates, leaving a sweet, rich taste. Rum cake is probably one of the better-known recipes in which the alcohol is used. Marinades for beef, chicken, fish, and shellfish are also common. Drinks, though, are its most popular destination.

One of the most popular, the daiquiri, is made from rum and fruit juice. The original Latino version used lime or lemon juice, but over the years, other fruits crept in. Now there are strawberry or peach daiquiris and piña colada daiquiris. TGI Fridays®, Bennigans®, and Houlihans® each offer them. And, like margarita mixes, you can purchase ready-made daiquiri mix (without rum) just about anywhere.

Those who don't desire the added calories or potentially dangerous effects of alcohol can also enjoy a rum-free version of this drink. Virgin strawberry daiquiris are particularly popular with children and teens. For a frozen treat, just add ice to a store-bought mix and blend it in a blender.

There's nothing like a virgin, frozen daiquiri or margarita on a hot summer day. The two drinks have become as popular as watermelon at a picnic. You can easily order both drinks in every state and province of North America, and both are the result of Latino influence on America's taste buds. It all started with tequila and rum.

> *marinades:* sauces, usually acidic, in which meat, fish, or vegetables are soaked to add flavor or to tenderize.
>
> *connoisseurs:* experts.

Beer and Wine

The most common alcoholic drink in Mexico is the local beer, cerveza. According to many beer *connoisseurs*, Latin American beer, particularly Mexican, is uncommonly good. So

¡Arriba! ¡Arriba!

One Salvadoran competitor of Mexico's Corona® beer noticed the huge popularity among Americans of the long-necked bottles and gold-colored brew. So the company stopped using its squatter, dark bottles and tried to pick names of the beers from Spanish words with which most Americans would be familiar and could easily say. The makers ultimately chose "Arriba" for their Safeway® beer because they thought most Americans would remember the cartoon mouse Speedy Gonzalez, who cried, "Arriba! Arriba!"

good, in fact, that some of the best brews are exported extensively to the United States and Canada.

But Mexican beer—unlike lemonade, coffee, tequila, and rum—has little that is truly Latin American about it. German companies run most of the Latin American breweries, and those that are run locally (or otherwise) generally follow German traditions, like many breweries in the United States do. Yes, native grains grown in Latin American soil are the ingredients from which Latino beers are made, but the beer is as German in character as if it were brewed in Munich.

Latin American beer imports now overwhelm many distributors' shelves. Mexican beer is the fastest growing import in the American beer industry, with a lighter beer leading the way: Corona®. Other labels include Chihuahua, Pacifico, Sol, Dos Equis, Carta Blanca, Tecate, Bohemia, and Negra Modelo. You can find them almost wherever beer is sold.

Then there's the wine market. The truly chic are increasingly sipping on Chilean, Argentine, and other South American wines. One New York restaurant boasts more than six hundred labels, all from that region alone. (Move over California!) As with rum, Latino wines are impacting our culinary habits through sautés and marinades, as well as straight from the glass.

Moving On

Clearly our southern neighbors (and millions of Hispanic Americans) are influencing what we drink. From lemonade to lime daiquiris, refreshment has never been more fun! For that we can thank the Latino community.

In the next chapter we'll look at Latino influences on the foods we use at home, school, and work. You'd be surprised how many restaurant trends trickle into everyday eating habits. Let's take a look.

Habla Español

arriba (ah-ree-bah): up

cerveza (sare-vay-sah): beer

vino (vee-no): wine

beber (bay-bare): to drink

tengo sed (tane-go sade): I'm thirsty

Latino Cuisine

7

Influence: Hitting Home

It's soccer night. That means home at three, piano at four, homework 'til five, get dressed for the game, then get to the fields by 5:30 P.M. How does a family squeeze dinner somewhere in all that?

Lots of ways! Thanks to the explosion of Mexican foods in the fast-food industry, more and more of the most popular "utensil-free" dishes (those you eat with your hands) are making their way to freezers near you. Frozen burritos, quesadillas, tacos, enchiladas, and a host of other offerings are just a grocery store away. That's no accident.

Latino Cuisine

Consumers enjoy Latino foods

polling: questioning people to determine opinions.

Grocery stores use a variety of methods to determine what foods they stock. One method is market surveys. Each year a number of research organizations and periodicals conduct consumer surveys *polling* actual spending practices, needs, likes, and dislikes among consumers (people who use and buy products). This type of market research occurs periodically in every industry. That's how companies know what to offer and when to offer it. The food industry is no different.

For example, every year the Institute of Food Technologists publishes a review of current food trends, including what American families are buying and eating. They get this information through surveys. Groups

In 2003, according to the Institute of Food Technologists, a few of the top-ten trends included:

- Heat-and-eat, ready-to-eat meals for busy families. (#1) (Translation: stock more meal kits with disposable utensils or hand-eaten items kids can wolf down in the car.)

- Everyday gourmet foods with casual comfort foods. (#3) (Translation: stock greater variety of gourmet foods or try unexpected combination-foods like dessert nachos [whipped cream, fruit, and sugar].)

- Choice! Choice! Choice! (#5)

(Translation: provide more exotic options in every food category, such as teriyaki apricot marinades or ethnic grain products like couscous and flax.)

retailers: businesses that sell to the public.

like the Food Service Industry, the Food Marketing Institute, and the Food and Drug Administration do, too. Countless organizations conduct this kind of research. These are merely a few.

Once the information is gathered, the research company pulls it all together and publishes a report. Grocery stores, restaurants, vending machine suppliers, and other food-service organizations line up for copies hot off the presses. Why? Because they all choose their inventory very strategically; they want to offer only those items they know will sell well. Surveys allow them to see what those items are. Such research provides valuable information regarding what people are currently looking for and, on the other hand, what people don't want anymore.

Granted, trends take a while to reach the nation's more rural areas. (If you live in rural Montana or Saskatchewan, don't be surprised if such products sound completely strange to you.) Believe it or not, the products mentioned previously are already common in our cities and larger suburbs. That's where trends start. How do we know? Surveys!

Food Service Industry News reports that the top-four food attributes consumers are looking for in the twenty-first century (after taste, of course!) are: (1) ready-to-eat, (2) heat-and-eat, (3) pre-packaged or on-the-go, and (4) no-utensils-required. *Resources*, another trade publication, reports that people want food that is fast and fresh. Heat-and-serve products topped their list, too. Those surveyed also wanted more foods to eat in the car or at their desks. (According to the report, hand-held foods will reach $2 billion in sales this year!)

Are you starting to see a pattern? So, too, are the *retailers* who study these surveys. Today's consumers are overworked. One in four women work more than forty hours per week.

More and more Americans are enjoying traditional Hispanic fruits like mangos.

Fun Facts

According to the National Association of College and University Food Service:

- Sixty-five percent of workers eat hand-held meals (like wraps or sandwiches).
- Twenty percent of take-out meals are eaten in the car.
- Home still ranks as Americans' favorite place to eat.

These days, both men and women must help with the care of home and family, run errands, and shop for groceries. Food that is fast, portable, and no clean-up, is hugely in demand.

SuperMarket Research, a publication of the Food Marketing Institute, also recently reported,

> The growth in diversity in the American population is reflected in the taste of consumers for more variety and more ethnic foods. Whether it's shopping at the grocery store or eating out, more Americans are opting for flavors beyond plain American fare.

First, we see a need for quick, easy, and clean. Next, we see a desire for ethnic cuisine. If you were a grocer, what would you conclude you should do as a result of this information? Address both needs in one swoop: carry more pre-made, ready-to-eat foods of varying cultures.

That's where Latino influences come in. Latin American cuisine is now one of the leading ethnic foods in the frozen-food market. In fact, according to the American Frozen Food Institute and AC Nielson, Mexican frozen entrees came in second only to Italian frozen entrees, reaching sales of almost $.5 billion just in 2001. Grocery stores know what Americans want, and they want Mexican.

The major food producers have been aware of this shift for several years now. These companies know that today's consumers are food savvy, having developed a taste for ethnic foods due to increased travel, frequent dining out, and having access to information about food on TV and the Internet. In addition, a continuous migration of people to the United States has created generations of immigrants, some of whom opened restaurants, which further influenced a love of ethnic food.

Automatic Merchandiser, another trade publication, reports that 31 percent (almost one third) of the $7.2 billion frozen, prepared-foods market belongs to ethnic foods. Within that segment, Mexican entrees posted the greatest gains. According to AC Nielsen, sales rose 20.6 percent to reach $448 million.

How did Americans move from meat and potatoes at dinnertime to tacos? They simply liked the ethnic flavors of the foods they ate out and wanted to be able to enjoy them at home—and they no longer had time to cook a pot roast! The progression, then, is something like this:

1. Immigrants arrive.
2. They share native cuisine with local people.
3. Local people like it and desire more.
4. Restaurants offering ethnic cuisine open and thrive.
5. More restaurants open. More people are exposed to the cuisine and like it.
6. Customers want to be able to make and eat similar foods at home.
7. Grocers learn of the need via market surveys.
8. Grocery stores stock both the ingredients for cooking ethnic meals and/or frozen, ready-made ethnic meals.
9. Consumers are happy! They stock up, and grocers are happy.

$7.2 Billion Frozen, Prepared-Foods

31%

69%

☐ Other ■ Ethic Food

Our modern lifestyle leaves less time for cooking meals.

Salsa and chips are a favorite snack.

This process works the same for any ethnicity: Chinese, Vietnamese, Indian, whatever. But if you have any doubt about the influence of Latino cuisine on the frozen food industry, just check your grocer's frozen-food section. There you'll find frozen enchiladas, burritos, quesadillas, taquitos, chimichangas, and even Southwest egg rolls.

Some products are the actual foods you'd buy at an established chain restaurant, simply frozen and packaged for sale. TGI Friday's and Taco Bell, for example, each have a line of frozen foods. Others are strictly grocery-store brands (like El Monterey and José Olé).

Sure, there are a lot of frozen dinners available now. That's easy to see. What about other areas of home shopping? How has the Latin explosion impacted everyday items like bread, canned goods, and snacks?

Snacks

It's Super Bowl Sunday, and you're expecting several friends for the game. Actually, you're not that interested in the game; instead, you and your friends can't wait for the commercials. It's become a tradition! Either way, you need munchies. They're just as much a part of the day as the game itself. What should you serve?

More and more, the answer is tortilla chips and salsa—and both are Latino in origin. Why these two foods have become so popular, particularly for football season and Super Bowl parties, no one is quite sure. Advertising over the years may have played

Happy Days Are Here Again

California Creative Foods began in 1984 as a small family business making Chachies salsa. They are now a leading producer of home salsas, with products in all fifty states. Does the name Chachies sound familiar? It should. The owner's daughter came up with the name after the popular *Happy Days* TV character Chachi, played by Scott Baio.

into it, but how it happened doesn't really matter. These snacks are here to stay!

Just look at the enormous success of salsa. (Salsa is the Spanish word for sauce.) When salsa first outsold ketchup—a strictly American creation—by $40 million in 1991, the *Times* ran the story on the front page. That's how big it was. Since then salsa and ketchup have been running neck and neck. One year salsa is number one; the next, ketchup reclaims its throne. And so it goes, back and forth. It's a condiment war.

Latino Cuisine

Salsa

Pop into any store and take a quick glance at the salsa aisle compared to the hasn't-changed-much-in-twenty-years ketchup shelf. You'll see ample witness to this phenomenon. We can't get enough of the stuff. Americans bought $924 million worth of Mexican sauces in 2002, according to AC Nielsen.

Even American icon Campbell's Soup Company joined the salsa craze. In 1994, the company most synonymous with the all-American kitchen for over 125 years acquired Pace Foods Ltd., the world's largest producer of Mexican sauces. Talk about Latino influence on American cuisine! The company retained the Pace name and continues to produce Pace salsas and picante sauces under Campbell's ownership. (Picante is a Spanish word that means biting or highly seasoned.)

Clearly, salsa—a strictly Mexican creation—is becoming as American as apple pie. Part of its popularity might be its diversity; the myriad brands have little in common besides tomato and salt. Just look at the jars at your local food store. Dozens of names jump out at you: Tostitos, Chi Chi's, Pace, Newman's Own, Dessert Pepper Trading Company, Chachies, Green Mountain Gringo, Walnut Acres, Jardine's, Martins, Herrs, Utz, and even Snyder's (a regional pretzel company).

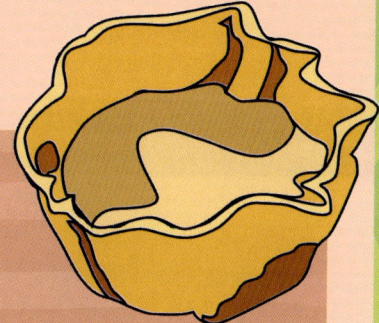

Fun Fact

- Ninety-three percent of Americans snack.
- Fifty percent of Americans snack two or three times per day.
- Thirty-seven percent snack four times per day.
- Thirteen percent snack five or more times a day.

Latino Cuisine

Tortilla chips

Because there is no "right" way of making them, salsas have limitless possibilities. They can be made of fruit (a Caribbean contribution), vegetables, a mix of both, or a single ingredient. The varieties of ingredients and textures are limited only by a cook's imagination. The defining factors are fresh ingredients and spices.

What about the chips? Move over, potato chips! Tortilla chips are as common as salsa, and just as varied. They come in bite-sized, restaurant-style, and even scoops; triangular chips are a bit more popular than round ones. Corn is the common factor, although you will see white-, yellow-, and even blue-corn varieties.

A restaurant worker prepares ingredients for tacos.

Influence: Hitting Home

Brand names of tortilla chips are as abundant as those for salsa. Dozens exist, too many to list here. And variations on seasonings are equally diverse. It's not uncommon to see such flavors as salsa and lime, nacho cheese, Mexican cheddar, hint of lime, or even black bean. Pringles—yes, the chip-in-a-can—has even entered the tortilla-chip race with its own version: Pringles Torengos.

But you don't have to be selling tortilla chips and salsa to know the influence of Latino cuisine on American snacks. It's everywhere. Jalapeño pretzels and jalapeño potato chips are now on the market. Bugles® offers nacho-cheese-flavored horns. Even crackers aren't immune. The makers of Cheese Nips® want you to try their salsa and jalapeño varieties.

Guacamole dips, cheese dips, and bean dips are stacked between rows upon rows of tortilla chips. And of course, there's Doritos®. Every kid knows that name. American snacking will never be the same.

Home Cooking

Jack had to take Home Economics and Consumer Science this year. His class just finished the sewing unit—and today is the first cooking class of the quarter.

"Okay class, we're going to start you off with something pretty easy," his teacher begins. "How do tacos sound?"

Jack glances at his partner. *Maybe this semester won't be so bad after all,* he's thinking. He loves Mexican food.

More and more households are discovering just how fast and easy much of Latin American cooking is. The ingredients are often cheap, too. Mexican food is a homemaker's dream!

Perhaps the single, most dramatic example of Latino influence on home cooking is the simple tortilla. We know now that salsa outsells ketchup, right? Did you know that tortillas outsell bagels? White bread may be next.

A Royal Gift?

According to an ancient Mayan legend, a peasant invented the corn tortilla as a gift for his king. True or not, the corn tortilla has been around for a very long time.

Workers' Wrap

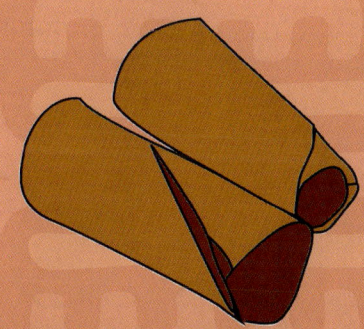

The flour tortilla originated either in Texas as a convenient food during round-ups or in northern Mexico as a practical way of getting beans to people working in the mines or fields. No one knows for sure.

versatile: *capable of adapting to changing conditions.*

Sales of the unassuming but *versatile* flatbread are catching up to the American-of-all-American-icons: white bread. According to a recent article published in the *Seattle Times*, the tortilla will surpass white bread as the top-selling bread in America by the end of this decade. "Tortillas have seen a steady growth of ten to fifteen percent a year seemingly forever," reflects Irwin Steinberg, the founding president of the Tortilla Industry Association based in Dallas, Texas.

The popularity of "wraps"—the "in" name for soft tortillas—has helped. Chain restaurants like Subway® (currently marketing its Atkins-friendly wraps) increased exposure of the bread to mainstream America. Then creative tortilla flavors like sun-dried-tomato-basil, basil-garlic, jalapeño-cilantro, and garden-spring-vegetable started showing up on grocery store shelves and made the eating adventure that much more interesting.

Frankly, many people are bored with their plain, old, white loaf—and tortillas have caught their attention. U.S. consumers now scoop up about $4 billion in packaged tortillas annually. That number is expected to increase to $6.1 billion next year.

American public schools recognized the benefits of such budget-friendly, convenient foods years ago. Deb, a forty-something mom raised in the Southwest, recalls, "Every Wednesday at our school was Mexican food day." And that was in the 1970s; now assorted wraps and soft tacos are common lunchroom fare, even on the East Coast.

Wraps can be rolled around anything. Traditional Mexican dishes would suggest refried beans and cheese or grilled meats and peppers. Americans, though, put whatever they fancy on them: turkey and cheese with lettuce, tomato and ranch dressing; grilled

Influence: Hitting Home

A Latino woman prepares traditional foods.

A taco salad—a salad in a tortilla

Italian veggies with onions and marinade; cucumbers and egg salad; even humus (a traditional Indian food) with sweet peppers. The point is that a tortilla can roll up around anything you can put on a sandwich.

Such versatility is one of the reasons tortillas are fast becoming a mainstay of the American diet. Traditional fillings are equally varied and easy to make. Just pan-fry some chicken strips and sweet peppers, and you have a fajita. Warm-up some canned, refried beans, add some shredded Monterey Jack cheese, and there you have it: a burrito. No wonder even kids are cooking Mexican at home these days!

Clearly, home-cooked Latino meals are on the rise. Refried beans, or the red beans with which they're made, line store shelves like a Mexican army. Bush's (the baked bean company, another American icon), Goya, Centos, and Eden's are just a few of the brand names touting Mexican beans. Black beans sport names like *frijoles negro* (Spanish for black beans), as though we needed reminding of their heritage.

French's (the mustard folks) makes seasonings and seasoning kits to spice up those beans. Hot sauces complete the same goal, and we've already discussed how that section

There are many Hispanic foods for sale.

of your grocery store has grown. There are countless blends and brands with which to add flare to your meal. Shelf space for such Latin American foods now surpasses that of Asian in many markets.

Where Do We Go from Here?

Since that first tamale stand opened in 1926, the impact of Latino cuisine on mainstream American taste buds is undeniable. Whether it's fajitas at TGI Friday's or burritos at McDonalds; or hot sauces at Taco Bell; lemonade at picnics or coffee at work; tacos at school or salsa and chips at home, Latin American food has influenced the way we wine, dine, and cook. Latino cuisine is here to stay.

Latino Cuisine

Across America, Latino restaurants offer delicious, fun fare.

Keep in mind that what's ethnic today will likely become mainstream tomorrow. In fact, in some areas, Mexican and Caribbean foods have been around so long that they're no longer considered "ethnic" like Chinese or Indian food. South American coffees are now a mainstay. Even the tequila-based margarita has become as American as soft drinks. That means that the currently obscure or yet-to-be-discovered next Latino trend will be an upcoming American tradition. Keep your eyes out for it!

We owe a great debt of gratitude to American Latinos and Latin Americans worldwide. The America we know today wouldn't exist apart from our friends south of our borders. They have generously shared the food and culture of their lands—and we're a much more interesting and flavorful country for it. Olé!

Habla Español

barrio (bah-ree-oh): neighborhood

salsa (sahl-sah): sauce

escuela (ace-cwae-lah): school

frijoles (free-hole-ace): beans

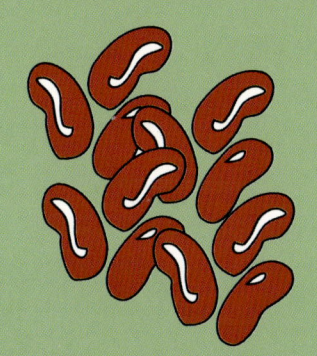

Timeline

October 12, 492—Christopher Columbus arrives in the Indies.

1519—Hernan Cortés arrives in Central Mexico.

1520s—Pedro de Alvarado arrives in Guatemala

1532—Francisco Pizarro arrives in Peru.

1700s—Filtering of coffee through cloth originates in Europe.

1720s—French sailor Gabriel Mathieu de Clieu brings the first coffee plant to Latin America.

May 5, 1862—Mexico defeats French to gain its independence.

May 10, 1893—U.S. Supreme Court rules that tomatoes are vegetables (though botanically a fruit).

April 25, 1898–December 10, 1898—Spanish-American War.

1926—First tamale stand opens in the United States.

1940—El Chico Restaurant opens in Texas.

1952—First Taco Bell (Taco Tia) opens in California.

1960s—Cubans, Dominicans, Colombians, and Costa Ricans arrive in the United States in mass.

1964—First Del Tacos opens in California.

1974—Jimmy Buffett's song "Margaritaville" hits the top of the charts.

1976—First Chi-Chi's opens in California.

1977—Chili is made the state dish of Texas.

mid-1990s—Sales of salsa surpass those of catsup.

2000—Latinos are the largest minority in the United States.

Further Reading

Bayless, Rick. *Mexico One Plate at a Time*. New York: Scribner, 2000.

Feniger, Susan. *Mexican Cooking Essentials for Dummies*. Philadelphia, Pa.: Courage Books, 2002.

Figueredo, D. H. *The Complete Idiot's Guide to Latino History and Culture*. Indianapolis, Ind.: Alpha Books, 2002.

Foster, Dean Allen. *The Global Etiquette Guide to Mexico and Latin America*. New York: John Wiley & Sons, 2002.

Jamison, Bill, and Cheryl A. Jamison. *The Border Cookbook*. Boston, Mass.: The Harvard Common Press, 1995.

McKenley, Yvonne. *A Taste of the Caribbean*. New York: Thomas Learning, 1995.

Novas, Himilce. *Everything You Need to Know about Latino History*. New York: Plume, 1998.

Pilcher, Jeffrey M. *Que Vivan Los Tamales! Food and the Making of Mexican Identity*. Albuquerque: University of New Mexico Press, 1998.

Rojas-Lombardi, Felipe. *The Art of South American Cooking*. New York: HarperCollins, 1991.

Sandovol, Richard. *Modern Mexican Flavors*. New York: Stewart, Tabori & Chang, 2002.

Tenenbaum, Barbara A. *Latin America, History and Culture: An Encyclopedia for Students*. New York: Scribner's Sons, Macmillan Library Reference, 1999.

Wade, Mary Dodson. *Cinco de Mayo*. New York: Children's Press, 2003.

Ward, Karen. *The Young Chef's Mexican Cookbook*. New York: Crabtree, 2001.

For More Information

American Demographics Magazine
www.demographics.com

American Frozen Food Institute
www.affi.com

British Coffee Association
www.britishcoffeeassociation.org

Canadian Federation of Independent Grocers
2235 Sheppard Avenue East, Suite 902
Willowdale, Ontario, Canada M2J 5B5

Canadian Federation of Independent Business
www.cfib.ca

Food Marketing Institute
655 15th Street, NW
Washington, DC 20005
www.fmi.org

Food Service Industry News
www.foodservice.com/news

Gourmet News Magazine
www.gourmetnews.com

Hispanic Online
www.hispaniconline.com

Iowa Division of Latino Affairs
www.state.ia.us/government/dhr/Ia/pages/News.htm

National Food Laboratory
www.thenfl.com

National Restaurant Association
www.restaurant.com

National Restaurant News
www.nrn.com

AC Nielsen
www.acnielsen.com

Prepared Foods Magazine
www.preparedfoods.com

Restaurant Business Magazine
www.restaurantbiz.com

Starbucks®
www.starbucks.com

Statistics Canada
Advisory Services
Discovery Place, #201
3553-31 Street NW
Calgary, Alberta, Canada T2L 2K7

U.S. Census Bureau
www.census.gov/

U.S. Food Service
www.usfoodservice.com

U.S. Citizenship and Naturalization Services
www.uscitizenship.info

U.S. Small Business Administration
www.sba.gov/

University of Iowa
www.uiowa.edu

Publisher's note:

The Web sites listed on this page were active at the time of publication. The publisher is not responsible for Web sites that have changed their addresses or discontinued operation since the date of publication. The publisher will review the Web sites and update the list upon each reprint.

Index

Africa (African) 20, 29, 45, 69–70, 73
alcohol 75–83
Argentina (Argentine cuisine) 12–14, 17, 24, 38, 83
Art of South American Cooking, The 45

beans 16–17, 23, 28, 38, 48, 59, 63, 97, 98, 102
beer 81–83
Belize (Belizean cuisine) 13–14
Bell, Glen 55–56, 62
beverages 63, 65–73, 75–83
Bolivia (Bolivian cuisine) 12, 13, 24, 45
Border Cookbook, The 28
Brazil (Brazilian cuisine) 12, 45, 46, 48, 71, 73
burritos 37, 40, 44, 49, 55, 59, 85, 92, 102–103

Caribbean (Caribbean cuisine) 12, 13, 17, 18, 38 39, 46, 48, 63, 66, 68, 80, 96, 105
Chi-Chi's 32, 34
Chile (Chilean cuisine) 12–14, 17, 38, 45, 83
chocolate 22, 28
Cinco de Mayo 79, 80
coffee 66, 68–73, 76, 82, 103, 105; brands of Latino coffee 73; chains selling Latino coffee 72–73
coffee-drinking habits in Latin America 70

Colombia (Colombian cuisine) 12–13, 24, 70–71, 73
Columbus, Christopher 18, 20, 66, 68
corn 17, 18, 23, 28, 29, 41, 48, 96, 99
Costa Rica (Costa Rican cuisine) 12, 13, 24, 73
Cuba (Cuban cuisine) 12, 13, 18, 24, 37, 39, 48, 63, 68
Cuellar, Adelaida 31–32, 34–35

daiquiris 81, 83
Del Taco 56–57
Dominican Republic (Dominican cuisine) 12, 13, 24

Ecuador (Ecuadorian cuisine) 12, 13, 37, 46
El Chico 32, 39
El Salvador (Salvadoran cuisine) 12, 13, 18, 24
enchiladas 37, 40, 85, 92

fajitas 37, 40, 44, 102, 103
fast foods 11, 51–63

grocery stores 11, 73, 79, 85–86, 88, 90, 92, 100, 103; examples of Latino foods sold in grocery stores 92
Guatemala (Guatemalan cuisine) 12, 13, 18, 24, 48, 73
Guyana (Guyanese cuisine) 13

Haiti (Haitian cuisine) 18, 68
Hispanic (definition of term) 11
Honduras (Honduran cuisine) 12, 13, 18
hot sauce 59, 60–63, 102–103

immigration 24, 27, 29, 35, 39, 90
Institute of Food Technologies 86–87

Jamaica (Jamaican cuisine) 12, 38, 73

Latin America (definition of term) 12
Latin American cuisines 13–14, 16–17, 35–36, 44, 46–49, 63, 90, 92
Latino; definition of term 11–12; influences on American culture and cuisine 9–12, 14, 24, 29, 35–36, 46, 49, 58, 72–73, 81, 83, 90, 92, 95, 97–98, 100, 103; leading cuisines 38–39; population and disbursement in U.S. 24, 27, 52
lemons (lemonade) 65–66, 68, 80, 81, 82, 103
limes 66, 68, 78, 83, 97

margaritas 76, 78–81, 105
McDermott, Marno 32, 35
McGee, Max 32, 35
Mexican cuisine 13, 28, 32, 34–39, 44, 52, 55, 57, 85, 90, 95, 98–100, 102, 105
Mexican fast-food restaurants 57–60, 63

Mexico (Mexican) 12, 14, 18, 20, 24, 29, 31–38, 47, 73, 78–82

Native Latin American people and civilizations 17–18, 20, 22–23, 45, 66, 76, 99
Nicaragua (Nicaraguan cuisine) 12, 13, 17, 24, 73
Nuevo Latino cuisine 37, 48–49

Panama (Panamanian cuisine) 12, 13, 73
Paraguay (Paraguayan cuisine) 12, 13
Peru (Peruvian cuisine) 12, 13, 17, 18, 24, 38, 45, 46, 48, 71, 73
potatoes 17, 18, 48, 90
Puerto Rico (Puerto Rican cuisine) 12, 13, 18, 24, 38, 48, 63, 68

restaurants 31–32, 34–39, 43–44, 46, 48, 51, 88, 90
fast-food restaurant "formula" 59–60
well-known restaurants with Latino foods on the menu 31–32, 34, 36–39, 47–48, 51–53, 55–60, 62, 81, 92, 100, 103
Rodriguez, Douglas 48–49
rum 80–83

salsa 9, 38, 41, 59, 92, 93, 95–98, 103
snacks 92–98
Southwest 44, 48, 55, 92, 100

Spanish conquest and exploration 17, 18, 20, 23, 45, 76
Spanish words often found on American menus 40–41
Suriname (Surinamese cuisine) 13

Taco Bell 55–60, 62, 92, 103
tacos 9, 37, 41, 44, 49, 55–56, 59, 85, 90, 98, 100
tamales 16, 32, 34, 37, 41, 57, 103
tequila 78, 80, 81, 105
Tex Mex cuisine 44
Texas 31–32, 34, 36, 99, 100

tomatoes 20, 22, 29, 41, 59
tortilla chips 41, 92, 96–98
tortillas 17, 28, 38, 41, 55, 59, 63, 98–100, 102
trends 60, 62–63, 86–90, 95, 100, 105

Uruguay (Uruguayan cuisine) 12, 13, 14

Venezuela (Venezuelan cuisine) 12, 13, 18

wraps 55, 100
wine 81, 83

Biographies

Jean Ford is a freelance author, writer, award-winning illustrator, and public speaker. She resides in Perkasie, Pennsylvania, with her husband of twenty-one years, Michael, and their two adolescent children, Kristin and Kyle. Internationally recognized, her work includes writing for periodicals from the United States to China, and speaking to audiences from as close as her tri-state area to as far away as Africa. Although she generally writes and speaks on nonfiction topics, Jean also enjoys writing and illustrating children's books.

Dr. José E. Limón is professor of Mexican-American Studies at the University of Texas at Austin where he has taught for twenty-five years. He has authored over forty articles and three books on Latino cultural studies and history. He lectures widely to academic audiences, civic groups, and K–12 educators.

Picture Credits

Benjamin Stewart: pp. 22, 26, 31, 32, 33, 36, 38, 43, 44, 47, 51, 56, 77, 78, 80, 92 (bottom), 94, 101, 102, 103, 104

Carin Zissis, carinzissis@hotmail.com: pp. 24, 25

Corel: pp. 10, 12, 15, 19, 62, 65, 88

PhotoDisc: pp. 85, 92 (top)

Photos.com: pp. 16, 23, 66, 67, 69, 71, 72, 75, 76, 96, 97

Promise Academy Center Library
641.5 F
Latino cuisine and its influence on American foods : the ta

T 92955